It's a good home.

There are flowers to sniff, a garden of carrots to fill my belly, a kind woman

and an old dog who likes to play.

Every night the kind woman and the old dog go into the house. Then I go to bed alone in my den. It would be cozier with a friend in my den to keep me company through the spooky night.

Sometimes, I daydream. What would it be like to have a friend in my den?

Oh, look! What's this in the garden?

It's a gift for me!

friend, just for me!

Now I have a friend in my den! His name is Mr. Lion. In his company, I am no longer alone. I feel safe and happy.

We spend each day doing all our favorite things.

Some mornings I go to the garden before Mr. Lion, the kind woman, and the old dog wake up.

This morning in the garden, I find something special! Can you believe it? Waiting there is another gift, this time it's for Mr. Lion too. It's too heavy for me to carry back to the den alone.

TO MARSHMALLOW AND MR. LION

My dear friend, Mr. Lion, and I will open the box together. I must tell him at once! He will be so excited to have another friend in our den!

Let's open the gift together.

...Nothing? There is nothing inside? How can this be?

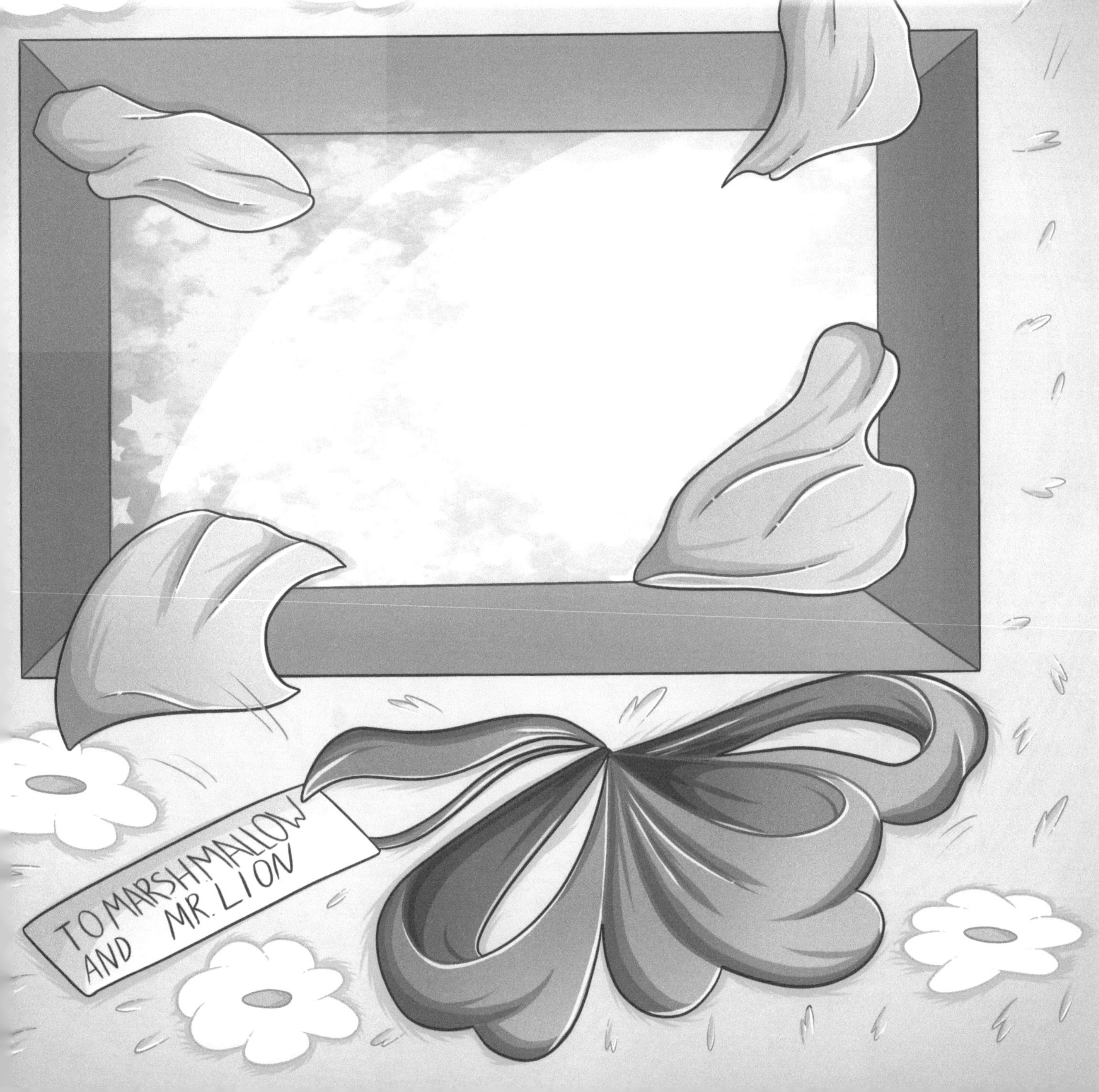

The gift just can't be empty. A friend is meant to be inside the box.

Even though I am sad, the gift box is special to me. It's a[ll]
I have left to remember the happy plans I made for m[y]
new friend. It's too important to leave alone in the rain.

The only idea I have is to plant the gift box in the garden.
If I do this, then the memory of the friend who never
came to play is with me forever.

"Marshmallow, the storm has now passed. Look up! Wha
a special gift your love has created for all of us to enjoy and
remember this friend by," said the kind woman.

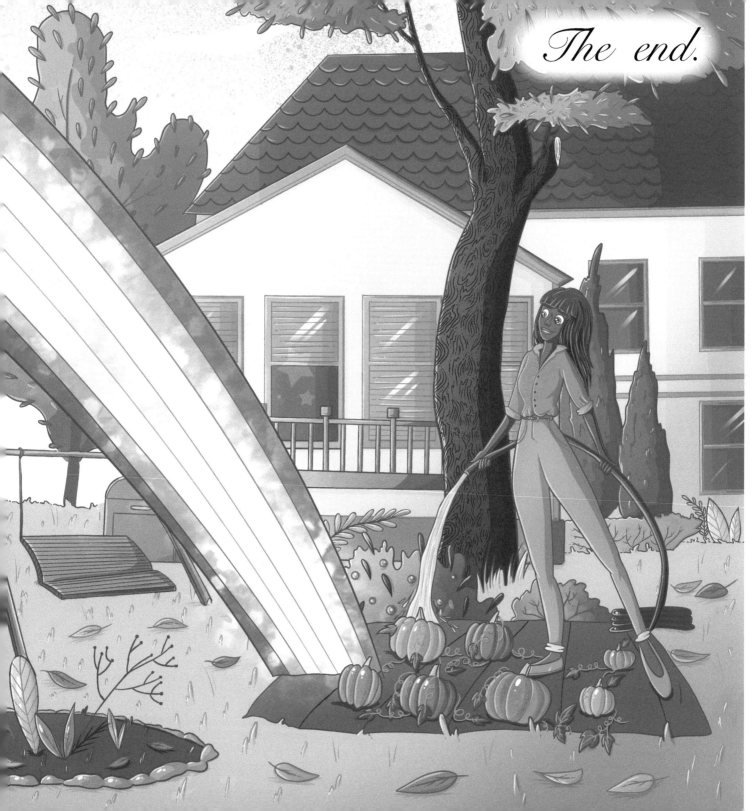

The end.

CPSIA information can be obtained
at www.ICGtesting.com
Printed in the USA
LVHW070115080222
710509LV00002B/20

9 780578 951560